Three Little Words

TROUBLED GIRLS FIND LOVE

KATHRYN REIGN

KATHRYN REIGN PUBLISHING

Copyright

Three Little Words

Cover Design by Les (germancreative)

Three Little Words

Three Little Words Blurb

I always thought Parker was the one, the other half of my heart, the one I dreamt night after night about raising a family with.

Until I found out that he'd been f*cking Stephanie... among others.

Fifteen years.

After fifteen soul-sucking years of being with the same guy, I now find myself **back in the dating world**.

First, it's Matthew, a data engineer whom I instantly connected with.

Until I stupidly said those three words, those **dreaded three words** that had him bolting out the restaurant doors.
I love you.

Guy after guy I'd meet, all heading for the hills.
Until Rodney Hersey comes along. Charming, sexy, and **he loves me back!**

Who would've thought?!

Immediately, I find myself dangling from his lips, tearing off my clothes, even getting married… after only one date!
But my life turns dark when I wake up in a strange home surrounded by four other women… *all claiming to be Rodney's wife.*

What have I gotten myself into?

A dark, short story about what happens when you say "I love you" to the wrong person.

Contents

Chapter 1   1
Chapter 2   11
Chapter 3   19
Chapter 4   31
Chapter 5   37

Stalk the Author   43

Chapter One

Fifteen Years. Parker had taken fifteen years from her. Fifteen years that she'd never get back. It all started when they were fifteen and entirely too young and too immature to see anything else past their lustful love for each other. They had been friends ever since the seventh grade.

Veronica had been seated beside Parker in their math class. She was always good at math, her mind proving to be nothing if not analytical. Parker, on the other hand, he preferred sports, history, and government.

"Hey, I'm Parker," he introduced himself. He was so lean and scrawny then. His voice was even higher pitched, as all the other middle school boys fell victim to, also.

Veronica tucked her hair behind her ear. "I'm Veronica," she murmured.

Parker leaned in close, closer than he should have with a stranger. He didn't seem to notice, but she did. She could practically taste the cologne emanating from his shirt.

"I have to let you know," he whispered, "I'm not very good at math. Never have been. So, I might have to lean on you a little."

Veronica could barely breathe. She thought back to that very moment years later and wondered if he was just using her from the beginning. Most likely, he was telling her this because he wanted to copy her answers. He wanted to give her a heads up that he wouldn't try to hide his need for "help." He probably wasn't trying to make a move on her or even flirt. But twelve-year-old Veronica ignored that. She was just happy to be spoken to. Especially by someone so popular, so charming, and so... good looking.

She let out a breathy chuckle. "That's okay. I can help you."

That grin — that wide, crooked grin as bright as the sun — with dimples lining each side in his rounded cheeks... she didn't stand a chance.

They bonded over math homework, juicy gossip amongst their friends, and after school sports. Veronica helped Parker with his math assignments, and if he fell short, she let him copy her answers. In turn, Parker invited her to his soccer games and convinced her to join him and his friends during their breaks. She helped him, and he helped her right back.

At first, it just seemed like a transfer of services. Parker needed help in class, and she could offer help. She was awkward and lonely without any real friends of her own, so he brought her into his circle. But as they spent more and more time together, she started to grow fond of him.

Parker was easy to talk to, something Veronica needed with her social anxiety and unconventional conversational skills. He was warm and bubbly and eager to draw her in closer. Even if his friends, especially the girls, weren't always the warmest toward her, Parker was always sweet. He smiled whenever they made eye contact in the halls. He laughed at all her bad jokes. He didn't tease her too much when she utterly failed at playing soccer with him one time after school. And her name on his lips...

"*Veronica...* I like you. Will you go out with me?" he asked her during their sophomore year of high school.

FRESHMAN YEAR WAS rough as they both adjusted to new schools, new teachers, friends leaving and new friends being made, and their interests dividing them more. Parker joined the varsity soccer team, something unheard of among most freshmen, and he was praised as a soccer god. He walked the halls proud, confident, and that grin of his drawing girls to him like the plague.

But it wasn't just his grin, his whole body changed when puberty hit. He grew nearly a foot, his voice deepened to a husky baritone. He grew out his hair so it hung in shaggy brown curls around his sharp jaw line and tanned face. After joining the soccer team, he started working out at the gym more, and he packed on lean muscle to accentuate his new physique.

He was the talk of the school, and Veronica fell behind, clouded over in the shadows. She joined the math team and the chess team, and quickly became a leader in their competitions. To help herself become more comfortable in social situations, she joined the debate team, too. That really forced her out of her shell and allowed her to make new, accepting friends. She was happy with this new life, and she was on a clear path forward, but something was missing. She figured that out whenever she saw Parker's bright grin down a packed hallway. He was never far away, but never close enough to reach.

By the beginning of sophomore year, she abandoned all hope that Parker would return to her life. But fate played games and had other plans for her.

One day during gym class, they were told that they would

be playing soccer. Veronica groaned, but everyone else started easily enough. Parker, as one might imagine, was thrilled, and he dominated the field. She tried to avoid him as best she could, but as her team climbed the ranks, and Parker's team had an obvious winning streak, the two met head-to-head in the final bracket.

Seeing as how she was useful in no other position on the field, her team deemed her their goalie. They did a fairly good job of keeping the ball away from her, and she was grateful. But against Parker, they didn't stand a chance. She tried to block his shots, and when that failed, she tried to confront him on the field before he reached the goal. But he easily went around her. He had no mercy, no compassion. Her blood heated, and she was determined to stop one thing that day. Even if it was only one ball, she would stop him in his tracks. She would show him and everyone else watching, that he was not unstoppable.

And so, she did.

Parker came sprinting down the field, soccer ball kept close to his feet. He dodged a defender, and then faked past another. He came closer and closer to the goal, and Veronica tensed. Parker's foot raised, and then the ball came flying at her like a bullet. She jumped in its direction, and she stopped it. Everyone went quiet around her; the light from the shining afternoon sun even dimmed.

She heard her name being called from somewhere in the distance, but her vision swirled and darkened at the corners as she tried to find the source of the deep voice. She could remember nothing from that moment to when she woke up later in the nurse's office, a thick bandage on her head and a chip in her tooth. Parker sat beside her bed on a plastic chair. He wrung his hands together again and again as his foot tapped on the floor.

She cleared her throat.

"Veronica! You're awake!" He jumped up, grabbing her hand. "Oh, God. Thank God! I was worried you'd never wake up after... well..."

Veronica touched her head as her last memory of the soccer ball flying full speed at her face flashed in her mind. She flinched at her soft finger's touch.

"What happened?" she whispered.

Parker rubbed at his neck. "I, um, I got a little carried away during gym class. The ball — it hit you on the head and knocked you out. The nurse... she thinks you might have a concussion. I shouldn't have shot that ball so hard. I hit you, and I hurt you, and... I'm so sorry, Veronica. I didn't mean—"

"Parker." She squeezed his hand gently. He peered down at her light touch. "It's okay. I'm alright. It was an accident."

Parker wavered, but she gave him her best smile, ignoring the pounding pain in her head.

"Okay," he whispered.

"Hey," she said, "remember when you tried to teach me how to play soccer in the seventh grade?"

He chuckled lightly. "Yeah. You weren't terrible."

"I was awful!" She laughed. "I tripped over the ball and fell face first into the mud. I could taste mud in my mouth for the next two days."

Parker's face split into a wide grin. His chest rolled with deep belly laughs. "Your face when you looked up at me — it was covered in mud. And that little glop dripped from your nose—" His laugh exploded out of him. "Oh, God. I couldn't hold it together. I felt so bad."

She smiled at him. Even if she had terribly embarrassed herself again in front of him, she was thankful to see his smile back.

After that, the two of them stayed camped out in the nurse's office until Veronica's mom came to pick her up two hours later. They chatted about school work, the classes they liked and didn't like, the people they called "friends," their extracurriculars, life at home... two hours stretched into an eternity, and yet was cut short. She could've stayed in that bed forever and talked to him. She missed his smile, his voice, his warm laugh, his teasing and jokes.

She missed him.

"Hey," she mumbled as her mom spoke to the nurse in the next room. "I, um, well, would you, um, maybe, you see, I—"

"Veronica," he cut her rambling short with a gentle smile. "I've missed you."

She swallowed past the lump in her throat. "I miss you, too," she whispered.

Parker smiled at her. "Can we hang out again soon? Can I text you?"

She nodded quickly, maybe a little too quickly. "Anytime, you know that."

She left that day with her mom and waved at Parker, thanking him for keeping her company. But that wasn't the last of them like she had half-expected.

Parker texted her that evening after school. And then the following morning. And then again during class. And then every moment of every day after.

They rejoiced like she had longed for, and then a week before homecoming, he met with her at the ice cream shop they frequented together. He bought a cone for her and licked at his own sundae. They ate in silence, and just when she was starting to think something was wrong, he took her hand in his, ice cream sundae forgotten completely.

"*Veronica...* I like you. Will you go out with me?" he asked her, his face abnormally serious.

She forced herself to swallow, but the ice cream burned with cold down her throat. She coughed and sputtered, and he handed her napkins.

"That bad?" He chuckled, but she could see the hurt

wavering in his eyes. She had never seen him so focused, so serious.

She waved her hands. "No, no! It was the ice cream. Parker, I... I like you, too," she mumbled.

Parker's smile blossomed. "You do?"

"I do." She blushed.

"So... will you go out with me? And, um... maybe be my date to homecoming?"

She nodded, not trusting her voice.

"Really? Really, really?"

She grinned then, the widest she ever had before. "Yes, Parker."

Parker scooped her into his arms and gave her the biggest bear hug. They finished their ice cream that night and talked in his car for hours afterward. They went to homecoming a week later. And then started junior year, and then senior. They went on countless dates. They hung out every chance they could. They hugged, kissed, and touched constantly. They were inseparable.

So, when they both graduated and found out that they were going to the same college, he asked her to move in with him, and she eagerly agreed. They finished college hand in hand and moved into their own apartment together after. Parker got a job in sports marketing, and Veronica became a data analyst. They bought new cars, they got a cat together, they filled their apartment with plants, with decorations, with love. And Veronica hoped that soon, they'd add children into the mix. It seemed inevitable. Almost as inevitable as the engagement ring on her finger now.

THEY HAD BEEN TOGETHER for fifteen years and had been engaged for one of those blissful years. Their marriage was

planned for the spring. She had almost finished the arrange-
ments and was finally starting to feel like she could relax and
breathe again. But just as everything settled, she found purple
lace panties in his sock drawer when she was putting away
their laundry. She dropped them on the carpet.

Purple lace panties — that were *not* hers.

She sat on the edge of the bed all afternoon, silently staring
at them on the floor. The sun shined high in the sky and flickered out into dusky shadows through the balcony door in their
bedroom. And then, the front door clicked, and Parker
stepped inside. He found her there, in the same position. But
he didn't need to ask what was wrong when he found where
her gaze landed.

"Whose are those?" she whispered, her voice croaking and
thick with held back tears.

Parker audibly swallowed. "Veronica..."

"*Whose*, Parker?" She cut him off.

He sighed as he slipped his work bag over his head. He sat
down beside her on the mattress and took her hand in his.

"They're Stephanie's, my... well, a woman I'm seeing."

Tears welled in Veronica's eyes. "Is she... the only one?"

At Parker's silence, she peered up at him. He flinched at
her gaze. "No."

"How long?"

"Nine months," he conceded.

He had been cheating on her with multiple women... for
nine months. While they were engaged. While she made
wedding preparations. While she planned on bringing up the
conversation of children... he was sleeping with other women.

She pushed herself up, wobbling only a little, and made
her way to the door. Parker grabbed her hand.

"Veronica, wait! Can we... I mean... is this it, then? Aren't
we going to talk about this?"

Veronica turned. She gave him the coldest, most distant stare she could muster. She wanted nothing more of him.

"You've made it pretty clear that this is it, don't you think?"

"Veronica, please. Let's talk about this."

She yanked her hand away from him. Parker's eyes widened, but she didn't care about the hurt she saw there. She just... didn't care anymore. She moved toward the door and heard Parker shuffling behind her, but he didn't go to grab her this time.

"Veronica! Please, just wait! Can't you just stop for a moment? Let me explain!"

Veronica propped the door open, her hand squeezing so tightly around the handle that her knuckles turned white as glue.

"I'm sorry I couldn't be enough for you," she let out. "But maybe Stephanie will be."

She clicked the door shut behind her and stepped down the hall. She left the shattered pieces of her past behind the door that day.

She didn't open it again.

Chapter Two

After being heartbroken by Parker, Veronica found it even more difficult than ever to meet and socialize with new, young suitors. Sure, she had bad social anxiety before, but after Parker's betrayal, she didn't know how to act around men. Was her flirting actually annoying them? Was her teasing too harsh? Was her quiet watchfulness not mysterious and humbling, but rather odd and awkward?

She had only one man in her life, one man to call her own — ever. Parker was her first everything — first kiss, first love, first roommate, and the one and only man she had ever slept with. He knew everything about her, and she him — or so she thought. She was comfortable with him. She came out of her hard shell for him, and she hadn't been back in since. But now that he was gone and out of the picture, she was left alone and confused.

She tried to talk to men at bars, and her friends from college pulled her along to clubs on the weekends. But as much as she boosted herself up and tried to fake confidence, she fell flat. The men she spoke to were nice at first, but the more she talked about her interests, her life, her past, and *Parker*... they put distance between themselves and her.

She reached out, trying to portray that fun-loving, friendly, carefree girl she had always been alongside Parker in high school, college, and then adulthood. But without him there, her crutch was removed, and she stumbled.

"Maybe you should try older men," her best friend, Maggie, suggested one evening at the club after Veronica had yet again struck out with a man.

She fumbled with her engagement ring in the front pocket of her bag. "I don't know. Maybe I'm just not cut out for dating."

"Nonsense!" Her other friend, Julia, yelled. "You'll find the right guy; it's just gonna take some time, girly. Don't let Parker and his wandering cock discourage you."

"But I just don't feel like myself. I can't talk to men, I've never been able to. Parker was a happy mistake, and he was the one who got me to come out of my shell in the first place."

Julia huffed, more than a little drunk. "*Parker* did nothing but tear your confidence down and make you question yourself."

"Yeah," Maggie chimed, sipping from her own drink. "You're better than that. You don't give yourself enough credit."

Veronica shrugged. "I don't know. Nothing I try is working."

"So, try online dating," Maggie said flatly. Both the other women looked at her. "What? Then you won't have to talk face-to-face with anyone unless you want to, and by then, you should have a better idea of what they're like and what they're into. Win-win."

Julia shrugged. "Not a bad idea, honestly."

Both her friends looked at her, and Veronica stared back as the gears in her head turned. She wouldn't have to go to clubs and bars and talk to total strangers. She wouldn't have to initiate conversation if she didn't want to. She didn't have to meet anyone she wasn't interested in. *And* she could talk to them anonymously until she was comfortable meeting up. Why hadn't she thought of doing this before?

"Let's do it." She smiled.

The three women downed their drinks after a short victory cheer. They left the club tipsy and stumbling over one another, but they quickly sobered up as they crashed on Maggie's couch in her apartment that evening. Julie got them all water bottles and snacks, and Maggie pulled up dating site after dating site. They worked together to make attractive, wholesome, and intriguing pages for Veronica, not without many snorting laughs and bubbling giggles.

By the end of the night, they had created three dating profiles for her on three different apps.

VERONICA FELL asleep on Maggie's couch that night and woke up the next morning to six messages from different men, all interested in her bio and wanted to get to know her better.

Veronica's lips curled into a smile as she scrolled through the compliments on her phone.

Her first in-person date with an online contact was with a man named Matthew. He was thirty-two, lived in the same city, worked as a data engineer for a large-scale company, and was into cheesy movies, hacking competitions, gaming, and robot fighting. He was smart, analytic, cute but in a nerdy kind of way, and very polite with every message he had sent via the dating app they used.

She was supposed to meet Matthew at a restaurant only a few blocks from her apartment. It was a small, local Mexican place that she suggested when he asked her to meet initially.

He agreed to meet her there at seven, so here she sat alone at a table, sipping on her glass of unsweet tea as the clock ticked closer and closer to seven. At five of, the door opened behind her. She glanced over her shoulder and, sure enough, the man from the pictures stepped inside. He ran a hand through his short blonde hair, and his blue eyes flickered around the main room from behind his round glasses.

She smiled and waved when she caught his gaze. He smiled right back as he sat down opposite her.

"Veronica?"

"That's me," she said lightly.

"It's a pleasure to finally meet you. You're even prettier than in your pictures." He flushed.

Her cheeks heated, too. "Thank you. You, um, aren't so bad yourself."

She eyed his tightly buttoned collared shirt that hung loosely around his lean chest. The golden watch around his thin, pale wrist. The blonde stubble that graced his jaw and neck. He looked like the opposite of Parker, but she still found herself attracted to him.

"So, you've been here before. What do you recommend for food?" He picked up the menu on the tabletop.

She pointed out two or three items that were worthwhile and recommended the house margarita if he wanted to enjoy a drink. He did, and he ordered exactly what she had told him to. She smiled at that.

"So, you're a data engineer. What exactly do you do?" she asked.

Matthew went into a long, drawn-out explanation of his job, to which any other person might have found boring, but seeing as her own position involved analyzing data, she was actually, honestly, interested. When he finished his rant, he asked her about her job, and she gladly told him about her work.

"It doesn't sound too different from mine." He chuckled.

She nodded, taking another sip of her water. "People always assume my job's boring and monotonous, but really, it's so interesting. I get to look for patterns in data, and from those patterns, draw conclusions that help consumers shop, and my company to better cater to their needs. I... well, I enjoy my job."

"I can tell. And I'm sure you're wonderful at it." Matthew smiled. "So, what else do you do, you know, outside of work?"

Veronica told him of her volunteer work, her tutoring of college tech students, her involvement in the local chess team, and about her outings with her two best friends. Matthew laughed at her story of the creation of her dating profile. He told her his and admitted much of the same issues that she confessed to. Dating was awkward, and meeting people was even more difficult than ever. Online dating took some of the anxiety off and allowed him to meet and greet people before meeting face-to-face.

Veronica was so happy to hear how similar they were, and after seeing Matthew's enjoyment of the food she also enjoyed and recommended to him, she was sure the date was going perfectly. They were in sync with each other — their hobbies, their jobs, their goals, their mindset... could it get any more perfect?

After dinner was finished, and the waiter cleared away their plates, Matthew offered to pay the check. Veronica said she should pay for at least some of it, but Matthew waved her off. He wanted to pay, he said.

"I want to treat you. And I'll have you know, this is the best date I've been on for quite some time."

"Me, too." Veronica smiled, her chest warming.

"I can't believe how in sync we are with each other. It's crazy, isn't it?" He laughed. "I guess it's a good thing that our friends made us set up dating profiles."

"Yeah," she mused. But she couldn't contain the happiness bubbling in her gut. It was all too perfect. Matthew, the restaurant, the food, the conversation, and for the first time in fifteen years, she was going on a first date, and that date was better than she could've ever asked for. And Matthew... she didn't want this night to end. She didn't want him to slip away, just as Parker had. It was all perfect — *they* were perfect together.

"Hey, are you alright?" he asked, eyeing her.

She brushed aside a few loose strands of hair and nodded briskly. "I'm just... thinking."

"About what? Enlighten me with that big brain of yours." He smiled teasingly.

Veronica took a deep breath and forced the words through her lips. "I think... I love you, Matthew."

Matthew's eyes widened. "What?"

She leaned forward in a rush, but he leaned away.

"I know it sounds crazy. I know we just met, but doesn't it feel right? I mean, we practically have the same career and are interested in all the same things. We're so *perfect* together. Don't you agree?"

Matthew's jaw dropped wordlessly. "Well, yeah. It's been really nice, and I'm interested in you, but we're still strangers. You can't... you can't love a complete stranger."

Veronica felt him retreating, she felt him slipping through her fingers, and she tried her very best to keep him from falling away.

"I know. I know! But I just... it all feels so right. And I just... I think you're the one for me."

In that moment, the waiter returned the check, and Matthew plucked his card from the sleeve. He stuck it into his pocket and pulled on his coat.

No... no, no, no! Veronica thought.

"I think I should go. This is... weird," Matthew said dryly.

"Matthew, no. Please don't go. Can't you see it? How perfect we are together?"

Matthew adjusted his glasses before pushing in his chair. "Maybe, but we can only really know that with time. And you just... told me you love me on the first date. Doesn't that seem at all odd to you?"

Veronica tensed, her shoulders painfully tight. "It's love at first sight."

Matthew shook his head. "For being so analytical, you're awfully romantic."

"Isn't that a good thing?"

He stared at her, his kind blue eyes now dark and cold. "Not if it's hopeless and unreasonable." He shook his head and stepped toward the door. "Have a nice night," he mumbled.

The door chimed, announcing his departure. Veronica sat there in silence, staring at the spot he abandoned until the restaurant closed, and she was asked to leave.

Matthew never contacted Veronica again after their date. So, she moved on to others. One after another, the men in her inbox dwindled. She went on five more first dates, and five separate times, she confessed her love to the men after realizing how perfect they were for her. Five separate times, the men looked at her with a mixture of shock, confusion, and pity. Five separate times, they left her there, alone, abandoned, and lovesick.

Maybe she really *was* a hopeless romantic like Matthew had said. But she didn't stop trying to find someone who loved her right back. That's how she found herself on a date with Mr. Number Seven.

Chapter Three

Rodney Hersey. His name popped up on her phone screen from one of the dating apps she used. Veronica eyed the incoming message. Did she really want to talk to a completely new man? Was she ready for yet another rejection? She stared at the notification and sighed. She swiped right to open it.

RODNEY

Hello, sweetheart. I hope this doesn't come off as creepy, but I matched with your profile and had to reach out. You are simply… stunning.

Veronica's cheeks burned bright red as she read the message over and over again. She clicked on his profile picture to open his page. He was thirty-four, a little older than the others she had looked at and talked to, but she didn't mind the four-year age gap. He worked as a travel agent but was very much a homebody. He enjoyed hiking, crosswords and sudoku, and cooking in his spare time. And his profile picture... Veronica stared for entirely too long at his face, taking in every detail.

He had light, fair skin and hair that looked black in the light, and pointed and poked up from his scalp in a perfectly messy attempt. His green eyes glowed in the sunlight, looking like glossy emeralds. His smile was wide and crooked, so very much like Parker's. But Rodney didn't have dimples like Parker. Instead, he had a tiny scar on the corner of his upper lip, the only blemish on his otherwise perfect face.

Veronica clicked back to her inbox and began typing a reply.

VERONICA

Thank you. I hope this doesn't come off as creepy, but you look like a model and way out of my league.

She hit send and immediately felt regret. Had she been too forward? Had she revealed her creeping on his picture? Did she seem shallow because she only complimented his appearance? What if—?

Ding!

She eyed her phone and saw the notification for a new message. She opened it.

RODNEY

We can both be creeps then. ;-)

She chuckled, but another message came through from him.

RODNEY

How are you doing today, Veronica?

She typed back.

VERONICA

I'm alright. Better now. How are you,
Rodney?

RODNEY

Oh, I'm just grand. Couldn't be better.

She peered at his picture again, butterflies lifting off in her gut.

RODNEY

Are you doing anything tonight, Veronica?

Her heart skipped at his usage of her name yet again. Something about hearing her name, hearing it on a man's lips, especially a man so attractive... she couldn't resist it.

VERONICA

I have no plans as of now.

She replied.
Rodney typed back quickly.

RODNEY

Dinner, then. At the Mexican place on the
corner of Center and 116th. Does that
sound good to you?

Veronica stared at his message. That was the restaurant she had chosen for her and Matthew's date. It was one of her favorites. But he couldn't know that, right? She scrolled up through the measly message history between them. Normally, she talked via messages to her potential dates before meeting them. Matthew and the others after, she had spoken to for at least a week before feeling comfortable enough to meet up. But this man, this gorgeous and charming man, wanted to meet her right away.

She was hesitant, as anyone might be when deciding to

meet a stranger from online in physical form. But something pulled at her, tugged at her to go, to meet him. She couldn't put a name to it, but she knew it was the right thing to do. She typed back her response.

VERONICA

Sounds perfect.

RODNEY

Great, see you then. :-)

Veronica looked at the time on the corner of her screen and found it later than expected. She rushed to shower, shave, pull out an appropriately outfit — something perfectly balanced between cute and sexy, and do her hair.

When she finally finished, it was 6:50pm. She raced downstairs and down the block to the Mexican restaurant. She crashed through the door at exactly 7:02pm, and it didn't take her long to find Rodney. He sat facing the door and looked up at her wild entrance. She smiled clumsily, expecting her tardiness and now messy appearance to put him off, but he smiled at her, his eyes gentle and bright.

"Veronica, so nice to meet you." He practically purred, his voice deliciously deep.

She sat down across from him and smoothed down her hair. "I'm so sorry I'm late. I lost track of time and couldn't get my unruly hair to work with me and... God, I'm sorry. I understand if you don't want to stay."

He raised a perfectly arched brow at her. "Do you want me to leave?"

Her eyes widened. "No! No, of course not."

"Good." He cut her short, his words ringing with authority. "Because it's okay if you were running slightly late. And it's okay if you're feeling a little flustered. Neither of those things would cause me to leave. I'm not that pretentious." He chuckled.

"Oh, well. Okay." She shuffled under the table, playing with her fingers on her lap.

Veronica suddenly found it hard to meet Rodney's bright gaze. It didn't just feel like any other person's gaze; it was hot and consuming. It felt like his eyes penetrated through her to her very core. She flushed red in the cheeks but looked up as he chuckled.

"A shy one, are we?" he teased.

Veronica's cheeks burned, but Rodney's gaze trickled down to her neck.

"I'm, um...," she cleared her throat, "so, you're a travel agent?"

Rodney smiled at her, the curl of his lips all-knowing. Up this close, she could just make out the scar on his upper lip that she remembered from his pictures. Even though he knew what she was doing, he allowed her to side track his attention from her rosy cheeks. He told her all about his job and how he enjoyed learning about different cultures and different people. And based on the information he learned, he designed unique itineraries and booked trips for others looking to get away. He figured out their needs and desires, and based on his knowledge, he created a memorable trip that catered to them.

Veronica nodded along and imagined herself on a plane to some far-off country. It would be good to travel, she thought. To get away from the city, to explore, to find herself again, and maybe, just maybe, she'd get lucky and find a sexy foreign man interested in her, too. She filed that idea away for later and smiled at Rodney.

"What do you do for a living?" he asked her.

She briefly explained her job and duties, and he seemed as fascinated by it all as she had for him.

"You're very analytical, then," he noted.

She nodded. "I always have been. But data and analytics aren't always right."

"What do you mean?"

She took a sip of her drink. "Well, I find patterns in data, and those patterns translate into some kind of conclusion. But when I take data from my own life, for example, dating — messaging guys on a dating app, meeting in person, having a great time, talking easily, meshing perfectly — all that data put together should equal something bigger. The conclusion would be that something *more* comes of it, right?"

"Right."

"And yet, when I take those next steps forward and reach for that conclusion, all the guys I talk to run away."

"What's the conclusion you've drawn?" Rodney balanced on his propped-up hand, eyeing her with sincere interest.

She swallowed, the lump returning to her throat. With her next words, this could either make or break the date. And based on past history and data, it would break it. But she had to try — she *had* to!

"Well, according to all my data, I conclude that I... love these men. I must."

"Hm." Rodney watched her. She expected rolled eyes, another man up and leaving after another failed first date. But Rodney made no move to get up. He watched her intently, that subtle, coy smile toying at his scarred lips.

"And what about me?"

"You?" She wavered.

"Do I fit into this pattern?" His eyes danced, but something darker, something hot and deep and powerful burned behind them.

"I mean, normally the data stem from all of my earlier conversations with these men. Before I met them in person. But you and I... haven't really talked much."

"So, you're stepping out of your comfort zone and analyzing new data."

Veronica eyed him, her chest tight and hot. What was happening to her? This wasn't the pattern; this wasn't even necessarily love at first sight like she had with all the others. But Rodney... he was attractive, flirty, a good listener, and genuinely interested. Should she reach toward a new conclusion?

"With the others... we talked beforehand and found similar interests. But you, you're so much different than me, Rodney."

Rodney's smile curled. "Is that bad?"

"No, just..."

"Just...?"

"New." Veronica admitted. "Unexpected. I don't really know how we would fit together."

"Don't know until you try, right?"

He took her hand in his and squeezed gently. His fingers were warm, lean, and tender. She never wanted to let them go. Rodney got it. He understood her like none of the others had. And even if he didn't fit her perfectly like a glove, even if his background and his interests were different, even if *he* was different — maybe different was what she needed.

Her chest tightened and heated as his gaze lingered. She could feel her cheeks burning again, but she ignored her shyness as she tucked a stray strand of hair behind her ear. Rodney watched her every motion. She wanted his attention on her; she never wanted to lose his gaze. And before she knew better, before she could even try to stop the words from escaping her, she blurted them out.

"Rodney, I... thank you for asking me out today, and thank you for listening. I, um, I really appreciate it."

"I'm as happy as you are to be here," he said. But as he

watched her, he tilted his head. "But that isn't what you wanted to say to me, is it?"

Veronica's gaze widened, but his lips curled into a tight smirk.

"Well, I..."

"You... what, Veronica?" he teased.

She squeezed his hand tight, and in a rush, everything came out. "I love you, Rodney. I... I know it sounds crazy, and you definitely don't fit my normal data pattern but... I just have this feeling with you and... well, I just—"

Veronica was cut short when Rodney stood from his chair, leaned over the table, and grabbed the sides of her head. He pulled her close enough to smell the mint on his breath. She shivered.

"I love you, too, Veronica," he whispered.

And then his lips crashed into hers.

They were hot and wet, and sucked impatiently at her own. She inhaled him in, basking in his scent, his taste, his presence over her. She let him take control, and he did so seamlessly. They broke apart for only a moment as he shoved money onto the table and grabbed her again to lead her outside. He pressed her up against the wall to the side of the building. She sighed and cried out impishly. Rodney took full advantage of her opened mouth, letting his tongue explore.

He pulled back after many moments and whispered in her ear. "Veronica, will you marry me?"

She paused, her swollen lips frozen in shock. He... this man — he wanted her? All to himself?

She nodded slowly at first, then faster.

"Really?" he whispered.

She pulled his face within inches of her own. "Bring me home and make me yours," she whispered.

Rodney needed no more motivation than that as he picked her up, bridal style, and threw her into a cab he hailed at the corner. She giggled at his dramatic exit, but once inside the cab, they were all over each other again. The night was a blur of sweat, moaning, intoxication, and pleasure.

It wasn't until Veronica woke up in a foreign bed the next morning, Rodney asleep at her side, that she remotely questioned what had happened. But one look at the ring on her finger, and all hesitation and denial flickered.

That was, until another woman, short, stout, and with hard features, stepped through the bedroom door. She stared hard at Veronica, still naked and wrapped up in the bed sheets.

"Your breakfast is downstairs, whenever you're ready," she said, her voice equally as thick and husky as she appeared outwardly.

Veronica watched her go in silence, the door clicking shut behind her. She stared at the solid wood before Rodney sighed out of his slumber beside her. He peeked an eye open and smiled at her.

"Hello, sweetheart. Sleep well?"

As he sat up and kissed her cheek, she felt nothing but a burning chill on her skin. She got dressed in her clothes from the night before, but her shoes were nowhere to be seen. When she asked Rodney, he said she wouldn't have to worry about wearing shoes anymore. She wavered, but he didn't react, so she followed him down two flights of steps to the first floor.

They stepped into a wide, farmhouse kitchen that she could only admire from the magazines she flipped through at the dentist. But she didn't even have a chance to admire this one because surrounding the kitchen, were four other women of varying ages, but mostly still young. They all eyed her with that same hard gaze that the first one had.

"Good morning, ladies. I hope you all slept well. Serena, thank you for the wakeup call this morning. I would have slept in until noon had you not come in." Rodney chuckled.

Serena, the woman who came into the bedroom, huffed out a forced laugh but didn't look away from her.

Rodney nibbled on a piece of toast before planting himself by her side again. He wrapped an arm around Veronica's shoulder and grinned, the crumbs of toast still dotting his stubbled chin.

"Ladies, this is Veronica. She will be joining us from now on. Veronica, meet Serena, Rachel, Nikki, and Quinn."

Veronica lifted her hand in an awkward wave, and the other women nodded silently. Serena stared at her harshly. Rachel looked younger than her with long dark hair, olive skin, and a chest many women would pay whole savings accounts for. Nikki was petite, pale as a ghost, with bright red hair that sprung off her scalp like corkscrews. She barely met Veronica's gaze. And Quinn eyed her behind glasses, one corner of which Veronica could see was broken. She was tall but unusually thin, like she might float away from the next breeze.

"Now, I must be heading off to work." Rodney glanced at a watch on his wrist. "But you ladies take care of Veronica and welcome her kindly, please."

"Wait, what—"

Rodney took her face in his hands and kissed her long and hard. When he finally came up for air, Veronica found that she couldn't get enough oxygen into her lungs.

"You be good now. I'll be home again this evening, okay?"

"But—"

Rodney kissed her forehead, not letting more words pass her lips. He made for the door and stopped at the opening.

"Welcome home, sweetheart." He gave Veronica one more tight smile, and the door clicked shut behind him, followed by six heavy locks.

Veronica stared after him in silence until Rachel touched her shoulder. She turned.

"Come on, let's get you cleaned up. Then I can show you around."

Veronica let the woman lead her to the shower, where she wordlessly cleaned her body, finding the marks and scratches all over from the night before. When she came out again, Rachel gave her a set of fresh clothes.

"But where are mine?" she asked.

Rachel pushed the thin, plaid smock into her hands. "It's better to get rid of them now. It makes it easier to move on."

"Move on... from what?"

"From your previous life."

"My... what are you talking about?"

Serena and the others stepped into the bedroom doorway.

"Your life is over, dear. You live here now," Serena said harshly.

Veronica couldn't swallow past the lump in her throat. "What does that mean?"

"You said yes to his proposal, didn't you?" Quinn chimed in.

Veronica nodded silently.

All the girls' eyes dropped like they knew too well what that meant.

"What?" Veronica asked, a well of panic rising up her throat. "What?"

"You accepted his proposal, dear. You're one of us now." At Serena's words, Veronica stiffened.

But she didn't have to ask what being "one of them" meant, because Serena wasn't the gentle talker in the household. She sat down on a chair in the corner of the bedroom and eyed Veronica. "You're married to him now. You're a Hersey wife. Just like the rest of us."

Veronica had to sit on the corner of the bed to avoid fainting.

Chapter Four

It turned out Rodney Hersey had five wives. And all five of them were trapped in this house under his orders. He came and went as he pleased for business and pleasure, but all his wives weren't permitted to leave the house under any circumstance. The only one who had was Nikki, who turned out to be shyer and more afraid than any of the others.

Nikki helped Rodney pick up groceries once a week. She went to the small local store with him, followed him quietly as he pushed the cart from aisle to aisle and made mindless, polite chit chat with other customers, and then helped him load the car and unload it once they returned to the house. She was the only one permitted to do this task with him because of her quiet, skittish nature.

Serena used to do it when she was the first wife, but after Rodney had gained more and more women in his household, she apparently went off the deep end and became wild in public. Thankfully for Rodney, people in town called her "crazy" and assumed, after her disappearance from the public eye, that Rodney had divorced her. Or so he told them.

Rachel was calmer generally, and friendlier than the

others, but she also had fiery fits. She was stubborn and strong-minded, making her impossible to bring out in public.

And Quinn — Quinn was quiet like Nikki, but she wasn't afraid or shy like her smaller, meek counterpart. Quinn was watchful, intent, and sharp, like a knife that could stab you in the back at any moment. She listened well to Rodney, as much as the others did, but Quinn always appeared deep in thought, like she was plotting something.

Veronica got along with the other four women well enough, but found it hard to empathize with them.

Why did they accept his proposal?

"I was in a hard place. My boyfriend dumped me, my parents abandoned me, I didn't have money, couldn't afford a place... Rodney showed up with a promise of love and care at the right time."

What did Rodney do to them?

"Nothing bad at first. We are expected to wait on him hand and foot, like maids. And most of the time, he's pleasant enough, mostly just creepy. But when he gets mad... that's a different story."

What did he do when he got mad?

"You don't want to know. Just don't make him get there. And if he comes home mad... stay out of his way."

Why didn't they try to get out?

"The house is locked at every entrance and exit point. All windows, doors, attic spaces, basement — and all the windows are made of some kind of unbreakable, sound proof material that's single-sided so we can't break ourselves out, and no one from the outside can see or hear us in here. There's no way *to* escape."

Why didn't Nikki say something when she was outside?

"Have you seen the girl? She's barely said two words to us, much less cry for help in public with the man himself right at her hip."

Why didn't they all overthrow him and get the key to escape? They outnumbered him; surely, they could win in a fight.

Serena shook her head sadly. "No, my dear, we wouldn't."

"Why not?" Veronica paced the kitchen back and forth, and back and forth, and back and—

"Because he has a gun."

Veronica paused. "Has he... ever used it?"

Serena swallowed, the bulge in her throat bobbing. She shook her head as her hand covered her face. Nikki stepped behind her and stroked her hunched back.

"He used his gun once," Rachel said from her perch on the kitchen island stool. "He only needed to use it once."

"What did he do?" she asked quietly.

Rachel eyed Serena before her deep voice whispered, "He shot Serena. And he killed another wife."

Veronica's breath caught in her throat. "He... he killed a woman?"

Rachel nodded slowly. "The last wife, the Number Five before you. Her name was Anna."

Serena choked on a sob, rough sniffling echoing in the silent room.

"What happened?" Veronica whispered.

Quinn chimed in then from her spot in the doorway, leaning on the frame. "Anna asked many of the same questions that you're asking, but she refused to stay here. She made a plan to escape and wanted to bring us all with her. So, she devised a plan, where we would attack Rodney upon his arrival from work, knock him out, get his keys, and then escape to the nearest house or police station to get help."

"So, what went wrong?"

"Rodney had a gun at his hip. Anna attacked from the front, and Serena attacked from behind. Rachel and I went for his legs, and Nikki hid because, well, we didn't want her to get hurt. But once we managed to get Rodney to the ground, he turned and shot blindly. It just so happened that the person in range was Anna.

"She collapsed and bled out on the floor right over there." Quinn pointed toward the front door, to which Serena's muffled cry grew louder. "We all ran from him in fear, and he came after us. But even after he rounded us up, threatened to kill us, and asked who had initiated the plan, none of us would crack. Until he turned the gun on Nikki."

"Nikki had nothing to do with the plan and had been hiding all along! He even found her hiding in the cupboard. He knew she was innocent, and he still put that stupid gun right to her head!" Rachel cried out.

Quinn hushed her, but Rachel was fuming.

"He threatened to kill Nikki if we didn't talk," Quinn conceded. "He was willing to kill an innocent woman whom he had stolen and hid away himself to begin with, all so we would be fearful enough to give him what he wanted."

Veronica glanced at Nikki, who had quiet tears running down her cheeks.

"But he already killed Anna. Wasn't that enough? You said she was the one who plotted the attack in the first place."

Serena lifted her head then, her eyes bloodshot and angry in the dim light coming in through the windows. "He killed Anna accidentally, but I don't think he ever thought twice about it. But Nikki, dear, sweet little Nikki had done nothing wrong and, still, he raised his weapon at her. That was a choice, one he was willing to make. So, we told him that I helped Anna plan the attack."

Veronica's eyes widened. "Did you?"

Serena's hard gaze didn't waver. "In a way, yes. In others, no. But I wasn't about to let that man kill another innocent woman just because he could."

"So, he... he shot you for it?"

Serena pulled down one of her stockings to show the

scarred hole in her calf. It was twisted and red and angry, even after all this time. Veronica's jaw tightened at the sight of it.

"Shot me in the leg. It wouldn't kill me, but it would make it so I couldn't run and couldn't escape even if I tried."

The room fell silent as Serena rolled her stocking up again. The tension was so thick that one could cut it with a knife. Veronica herself was shaking with a mixture of fear, anger, anxiety, and utter, uncontained hatred. She had known Rodney Hersey the shortest amount of time, but even then, the entire blissful night she had spent with him felt like a disgusting lie.

This man who had flirted with her, charmed her, reasoned and delighted her, made her feel noticed and loved—

He was a liar, a cold-blooded killer, an abuser, a manipulator, and psychotic if he thought he could keep her trapped here for the remainder of her days.

Veronica eyed Nikki, huddled around Serena, who held the fragile girl's hand with a thick, heavy grip of her own. Rachel, who sat hunched and fuming on the bar stool, tense with angry energy. And Quinn, who watched from a distance, cold, hard, and calculating, but unrelenting. Veronica took a deep, steadying breath.

"We should try to escape."

All the women looked up at her like she was crazy.

"Weren't you just listening? We just told you a whole extended story of why we *can't* escape," Quinn snapped.

"I *was* listening. Were you? Because all I hear and see are four strong women who have been beaten down, manipulated, and abused by Rodney Hersey. And while they made a stand, it failed. So, what? You're just going to give up? You're just going to live out the rest of your days in this house calling yourselves his 'wives' with no argument, no fight of your own?"

"He'll kill us all if we try to escape again, Veronica. It's not reasonable." Rachel scowled.

But Veronica wasn't so sure. "No. You just haven't studied him enough. You haven't collected enough data. You have to find the pattern first, and then build a conclusion."

The four of them looked at her like she had three heads. She sighed.

"We have to figure out his schedule, his habits, his preferences, the exact timing of his actions, and the choices he'll make when offered them. Only then can we make a foolproof plan. One that will grant us all our freedom and won't get anyone else hurt."

Rachel and Quinn eyed her skeptically. Nikki watched on in stunned silence, but it was Serena, with the hole in her leg, who stood up. She huffed, leaning awkwardly to one side because of her wound. But that didn't stop her from looking strong and certain as she met Veronica's gaze.

"It's time. We can't let him hold us down with fear anymore." Nikki nodded ever so slightly, and the other two, maybe out of surprise after seeing Nikki's reaction, nodded, too. "Tell us what we need to do."

Chapter Five

Veronica put the plan in action after a week of gathering data. With the help of the four other women, they tracked Rodney's schedule to the minute. They gathered his preferences in regards to women, situations, and entertainment. They figured out who he talked to and trusted more, and who could distract him if needed. They discerned from Nikki's memory from going to the grocery store how to get there, and figured it would be a good enough place as any to get help. They talked about his weaknesses, his blind spots, and after a week of digging and relentless flirting and nights in bed with all of them, they discovered his hiding place.

In the drawer of his nightstand. He put his watch in there every night and closed the door. After some spying in the middle of the night, Rachel thought he only put the watch there and nothing more. It appeared mostly empty.

But then Quinn found the lever above the top lip of the opening; there was a tab. When pushed to the side, a compartment opened up at the drawer's bottom. And inside, there were two keys. One was for the safe in the bedroom, which once they opened it, they found cash and ammo for his handgun. The other key was for the bedroom, need he ever lock it, which he hadn't, the women told Veronica, except for right after Anna's death. He had dragged her body into the bedroom and locked it up for two days. After he reopened it, Anna's body was gone, and in its place, were ten small garbage bags, reeking of something rotten and foul.

The women didn't ask any questions; they couldn't in fear of what the answer might be. But they knew; it was unavoidable with the stench that lingered for weeks after.

From this information, they created a plan together, and that evening, when Rodney returned home at exactly 6:02pm as planned, they put it into action.

Serena made them all dinner and had it prepared and ready on the table for when he showed up. He sat down with a smile and greeted them all like any other day.

"How are my ladies doing?"

They all smiled tightly, fingers fidgeting on their laps, and forks scraping food across their mostly full plates. But Rodney paid no mind. He talked about his day at work and complained about his boss, who apparently babied him "like the royal asshole he was." Babied him — how unfortunate for him, truly.

But as he talked, they all gave each other flickering gazes. It was almost time. He would be finished eating, and his plate needed to be cleared in three minutes. And it was.

He would then go to the living area and watch a documentary on something only he was interested in for an hour and a half. Rachel would offer him a drink, whiskey with a splash of Coke, just as he liked. But Serena's foul cooking, in addition to the liquor, wouldn't sit well in his stomach. But he showed no sign of it during the movie. It was still early though.

Then he would use the toilet, brush his teeth, and kiss all

of them goodnight before choosing one to go to bed with him that night. He chose Veronica, her flirtiness during dinner and sensual touching during the movie made her certain that she'd be picked.

He brought her into the bedroom. He laid her back onto the mattress. She curled around him with all the grace and sexual attraction she could muster, all while the plan burned in her mind, and the memory of Anna and Serena's injuries made her blood boil.

"Take this big thing off; it's poking me in all the wrong places." She pouted, tugging at his watch. He chuckled before sliding it off and into the nightstand.

She kissed him hotly, not giving him time to breathe. But when he finally pulled back for air, he looked pale.

"I don't feel so well, sweetheart. Give me a moment." And with that, he ran off to the bathroom, locked the door, and she could hear him emptying the contents of his stomach into the bowl.

Veronica made her move. She wedged the chair from the corner under the door knob and moved to the nightstand. She yanked open the drawer and felt for the tab. It flicked under pressure, and the compartment opened up. She grabbed the safe key and the room key but again, there were only two keys. She hoped he would put the front door key in the same compartment, but it wasn't there. She grunted in frustration and heard the toilet flush once.

In a hurry, she grabbed his watch, too, and closed the nightstand. She wanted to get the money from the safe, or perhaps the ammo, so he wouldn't have any for his gun. She hoped his gun might be in there, too, but he must still have it on his body, hidden somewhere under his clothes.

She ran out the door as she heard the sink turn off. The door handle jiggled.

"Veronica? I think the lock is jammed. Veronica? Are you there?" he called.

Veronica slammed the bedroom door shut behind her and lock it in place, just as she heard kicking and bashing from inside. She flew down the hall and down the stairs, where the others waited.

"Hurry!" Rachel called.

She threw herself down the last few steps and landed in a huffing heap in Serena's arms.

"He didn't put the key in the compartment. There's no key to the front door."

"Then how are we supposed to get out?" Rachel yelled. "And why do you have his watch?"

"He wears it constantly, and keeps it with his other hidden things. I thought it might be important!" Veronica yelled, panic rising in her throat as a roar echoed from upstairs.

"Veronica!" Rodney's deep voice radiated downstairs like a vicious beast on the loose. She shivered. They had to get out; they had to go... *now!*

Nikki watched them all silently, bouncing on the balls of her feet. But Quinn grabbed the watch from her hands.

"You're right. He's always wearing it. And it seems odd that he'd keep it alongside his keys. Maybe..." She turned it around and around in her hands.

"Talk, Quinn!"

"I'm looking... ah!"

She flicked a cap open and pressed a small button, and out popped a piece of thin metal. Veronica pulled it out slowly and, sure enough, it was a key. She slid it into the lock and slowly, too slowly, each lock clicked open one by one. A sigh of relief escaped her, but too soon.

The door upstairs slammed open, crashing against the wall, and angry footsteps pounded on the steps.

Nikki cried out, "he's coming!"

They all turned and faced the beast at the stair landing. He fumed, his once charming and beautiful features warping with rage.

"You! After everything I've done for you, you're going to try and escape again? Good luck with that." He gritted out, pulling his gun from his waistband.

Veronica and the others shrieked, ducking behind the half wall by the door. Only Serena stood firm.

"Your time is over, Rodney. Let us go."

Rodney laughed, deep, dark, and horrendously.

"You think I'd do that? Just like that?"

"You have no other choice. You let us all go now in peace, or the other girls will escape while I take you down with me."

Rodney stopped at the bottom of the landing, gun still poised. "You think you can take me on after what I did to you?" He huffed.

But Serena was prepared to fight this time. She hurled for his head and dodged the angle of his gun. He shot into the far wall, and the other four women screamed, but Serena wasn't going to let him hurt any of them this time. She tackled him to the ground and threw away his gun. He fought back, pushing against her weight, but Serena held firm.

"Go!" she called over her shoulder. "Get out of here!"

They all ran to the door as Rodney cried out in rage, but none of them could walk through the open door without their friend.

"We can't go without you, Serena!" Rachel cried.

Quinn teared up, sniffling and shaking like Veronica had never seen before. But likewise, it was Nikki who surprised them all and pushed them through. She nodded at Serena.

"Thank you, Serena. I'll get you help; just hold on!"

Serena smiled sadly as the four women ran into the darkness. They ran down empty streets and hurdled over curbs and hills, the wind on their faces stinging like a cold ocean. They ran and ran until they reached the grocery store, and then they ran inside. They called for help, they screamed for help, and within minutes, the employees called the cops, soothed the women in a back room where they insisted they'd hide, and then the police showed up.

The End

Stalk the Author

Website:

https://www.kathrynreign.com/

Facebook Page:

https://www.facebook.com/authorkathrynreign

Instagram:

https://www.instagram.com/authorkathrynreign/

Goodreads:

https://www.goodreads.com/author/show/21854875.
Kathryn_Reign

BookBub:

https://www.bookbub.com/authors/kathryn-reign

Three Little Words